Pete the Popcorn 2:
Popcorns Practicing Principles

Sarviol Publishing
Copyright © Nick Rokicki and Joseph Kelley, 2014

ISBN: 978-1494914851

Special wholesale and re-sale rates are available. For more information,
please contact Deb Harvest at petethepopcorn@gmail.com

When purchasing this book, please consider purchasing
an additional copy to donate to your local library.

THE Pete Popcorn 2

Popcorns Practicing Principles

Written by **Nick Rokicki & Joseph Kelley**
Illustrated by **Ronaldo Florendo**

Pound, pound, pound!
Pete the Popcorn heard the pounding on his porch. Peering out the peephole, Pete peeked at his friend Patty.
But Patty had a partner!

"Hi, Pete," called Patty as the front door opened. "This is my new friend, Percy." Patty pointed at the kernel perched beside her. "Hey, Percy. My name is Pete!" Pete smiled at Patty and Percy. Patty was perfect when it came to sharing her friendships.

"We were just going to 5th Avenue to purchase pencils for penmanship class," said Patty. "Do you want to come along?"

Pete practically pounced off the porch to join his two friends. 5th Avenue was where all the popcorns paraded through shops and stores, perusing all sorts of different products.

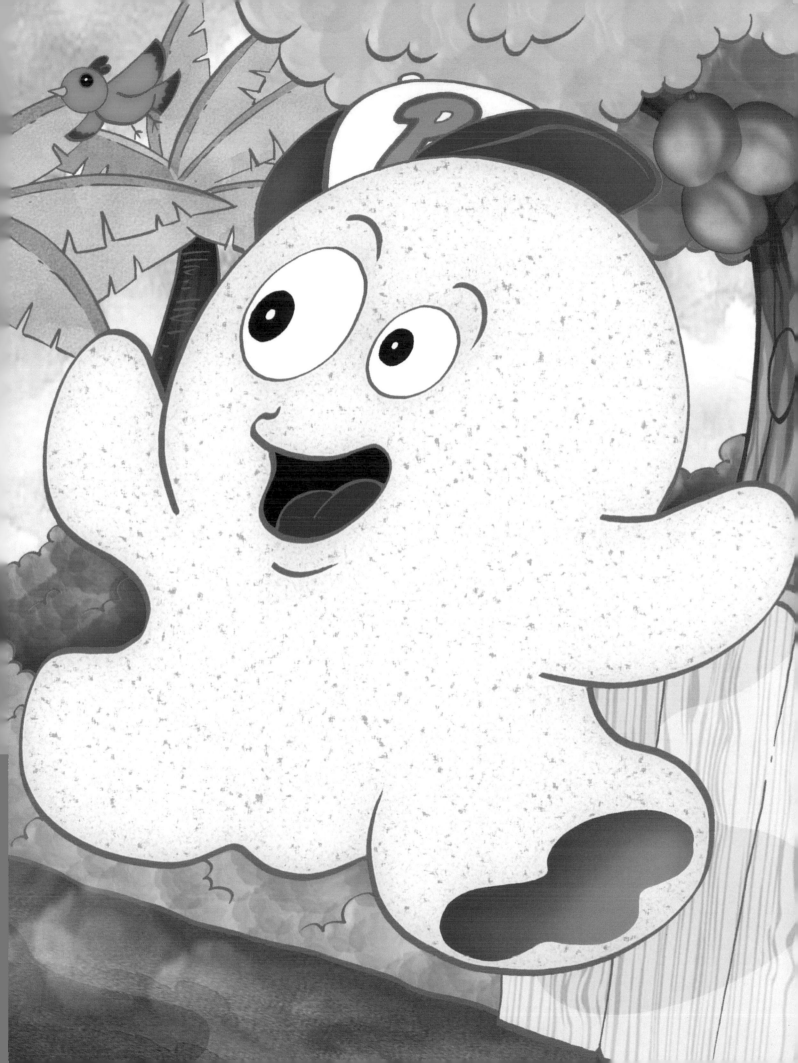

Pretty perfumes, pinstriped pants, perfect pots and pans, pink polka-dotted pajamas --- there was plenty to preoccupy a popcorn's mind.

Just as the trio turned the corner to walk onto **5th Avenue**, Percy proclaimed, **"look! A purple pocketbook!"** Pronto! Percy picked up the pricey parcel, pouting, "finders are keepers and losers are weepers!"

Pete looked at Patty. Patty looked at Pete. Pete and Patty pivoted to look at Percy. Precisely at the same time, they said, "that's not yours!" But Percy was already plucking through the pocketbook, looking at the owner's private property. "Oh, pooh-pooh," professed Percy the Popcorn with a wave of her hand, "this prize is all mine!"

Patty was **perplexed**. Pete was **panicked**.
The pair looked at Percy with painful faces.
Finally, Patty said, "Percy, sometimes it's pesky.
But us popcorns have principles!"

"That **pocketbook** belongs to someone else.
Put yourself into their penny loafers!
What if you were looking for something that you lost?
We have to find the owner!"

Patty's plucky pep talk had worked. Percy looked at the pocketbook. Then she passed it to Patty, saying, "you're right. Let's find the owner."
Pete grinned while Patty picked through the papers in the pocketbook. "Look! Here is a receipt, dated today, from **The Popcorn Cellar**," she said. "Let's take this to The Popcorn Cellar. Maybe they know who the patron was!"

The popcorns had a perfect plan. Now, all they had to do was find The Popcorn Cellar. The trio of friends walked down 5th Avenue, passing Pollyanna Popcorn's **Petunia Plantation**, Periwinkle Popcorn's **Pet Pantry**...

The Popcorn Cellar

Too good to let age

Pete the Popcorn spotted it first.
"The Popcorn Cellar! There it is,"
pronounced Pete.
Walking in the shop, the smell was pleasant
... pickles and persimmons! Pineapple and
pomegranate! Peppermint and pepperoni!
And popcorn, too! Shelves were piled with
pounds of popcorn, each in a painstakingly
pristine pouch.

"How can I help you little kernels today?" The polite voice of **Ms. Paloma Popcorn** sounded like a peaceful piano, thought Pete. Pete and Patty poked Percy on the shoulder, her cue to tell the story of the pocketbook.

When Percy was finished, Paloma Popcorn looked at the three young kernels and said, "I'm perfectly pleased with your performance. But we need to phone Police Officer Parker from Popcorn Precinct and report this missing pocketbook!"

Pete, Patty and Percy all watched as Paloma picked up the pink phone. They listened as Paloma painted a portrait of the pocketbook to Patrolman Parker Popcorn. A profound smile passed across Paloma's face as she put down the phone.

"The **owner** of the **pocketbook** was presently at the **Precinct** to report it missing! And she will be coming here to **retrieve** it, along with **Police Officer Parker**. They should be here any minute."

Pete said, "Patty, do you think we're in trouble?"

Patty said, "I don't know, Pete. I've never had to talk to a Police Officer before." Percy was frozen in place.

Soon, the picturesque door of The Popcorn Cellar opened to reveal Police Officer Parker Popcorn wearing his blue hat. Standing beside him was a popcorn that looked like a princess! Percy reached out to her, passing the pocket-book. She smiled and slowly said, "thank you so very much. I don't know how I'll ever repay you."

Patrolman Parker Popcorn patted Pete, Patty and Percy on the back and tipped his hat to Paloma, saying, "I don't think these little kernels are looking for any payment. They've learned a valuable lesson today: honesty is priceless!"

JOE KELLEY AND NICK ROKICKI

Joe and Nick are thrilled... and a little bit overwhelmed... to be releasing their 6th title for children. Their first book, Pete the Popcorn, debuted in February, 2012.

Their journey across the country, visiting with over 100,000 children in 25 states, has come full circle with this follow-up to their first bestseller. "After Pete the Popcorn, we've had countless teachers and parents approach us with lessons that they are looking for in children's literature. Honesty has been a big one... and that's what we are tackling with Pete the Popcorn 2," said Rokicki.

"While we obviously have fun writing these stories, the most fulfilling part of this whole experience has been the people we've met and especially ones that we now call friends. There is a sense of community that still exists in this country," said Kelley. "It is that sense of community that needs to be nurtured among our youth. Positive messages and learning how to encourage our friends and neighbors is the answer to so many problems. Nick and I are just starting where the biggest impact can be had: children."

To learn more about future projects, please visit www.PeteThePopcorn.com

RONALDO FLORENDO

Ronald is excited to have completed his fourth project with Joe and Nick. Taking the lovable character of Pete, who was still a kernel in the first book, and transforming him to a "popped" corn, was Ronald's challenge in this book. Currently, he creates illustrations for children's books full-time. In his spare time, Ronald enjoys spending time with his family, hanging out on the beach and at home playing billiards. To learn more about Ronald, visit www.Behance.net/RMFlorendo14

Naples Favorites

Special Flavors

Gift Packages

The Popcorn Cellar

TOO *Good* TO LET AGE

The Popcorn Cellar

To my Mom & Dad,
Thank you for teaching me
to work hard & always
do the right thing.
Im proud to be a Fortune.
Love, Patti

Made in the USA
Charleston, SC
24 March 2014